Snail and Caterpillar
Helen Piers
Pictures by Pauline Baynes

KESTREL BOOKS

KESTREL BOOKS
Published by Penguin Books Ltd
Harmondsworth, Middlesex, England
Text Copyright © 1972 by Helen Piers
Illustrations Copyright © 1972 by Pauline Baynes

All rights reserved. No part of this publication may be reproduced, stored in a retrieval system, or transmitted in any form or by any means, electronic, mechanical, photocopying, recording, or otherwise, without the prior permission of the Copyright owner.

First published in 1972 under the Longman Young Books Imprint

Second impression 1973
Third impression 1976

ISBN 0 7226 5269 0

Printed in Belgium by Offset-Printing Vanden Bossche

Snail woke up. He yawned, stretched himself, and peeped out of his shell.

It was a dismal, drizzly morning.

"It's very wet and swashy today. That's *nice*," said Snail. "I'll go and see Caterpillar." So, with his shell balanced on his back, he set off through the wet leaves.

It was a long way to Caterpillar's cabbage.
Over the nettles, up the stalk of the foxglove,

along the brambles to the wall, through the crack, and down the cherry-tree to the cabbage patch—it was a morning's journey for Snail. "No need to hurry," he said. "Caterpillar is always at home."

When at last Snail got to the cabbage patch, the rain had stopped and the sun was shining.

"Oh dear, it's very hot and parchy now," he said, "but, never mind, it's always shady under Caterpillar's cabbage. I'll sit here, beside the stalk, and cool off before I climb up."

But today it wasn't at all shady under Caterpillar's cabbage. Snail got hotter and hotter. He couldn't understand it.

Then he looked up at Caterpillar's cabbage. *And it wasn't there!*

Worm put her head out of the ground.
"They cut it off. Didn't you know? Poor Caterpillar!" Snail wanted to ask if Caterpillar was at home when it happened, but he was too late. Worm had gone under the ground again.

Snail crawled across the cabbage patch and into the grass. He was worried.

"Zik-zik-z-z-z-k!" Grasshopper jumped and landed on a blade of grass behind him. "They took it away, didn't they? Poor Caterpillar! Zik-zik-z-z-z-k!"

Slowly Snail turned round. He wanted to ask where they had put Caterpillar's cabbage, but he was too late. Grasshopper had gone, and was already dancing up and down at the other end of the field.

"That silly insect," sighed Snail. "He never keeps still for a moment."

Snail climbed a blade of grass and looked all around. He couldn't see Caterpillar's cabbage anywhere, but he saw Beetle scurrying along.

"T-t-t-t!" muttered Beetle. "That's what they are going to do with it, of course. T-t-t-t! Poor Caterpillar! Poor Caterpillar! I can't stop now. I can't stop now. I've got a lot of things to do. I've got a lot, a lot..."

Snail wanted to ask *what* they were going to do with Caterpillar's cabbage, but he was too late again. Beetle had disappeared under a daisy.

"Oh, why *is* everyone in a hurry?" sighed Snail.

Slowly he climbed down to the ground. If only someone would stand still for just one minute and tell him exactly what had happened.

"Buzz-m-m-m! Yes, I'll have a little of this. Buzz-m-m-m!" Bumble Bee was in a dandelion high above Snail's head.

"Oh, I'll ask Bumble Bee to tell me," said Snail. "She knows everything about everything— and *she* stands still when she's collecting pollen." As quickly as he could he climbed up the dandelion stalk, but just as he was nearly there, Bumble Bee flew away to a willow herb. Snail sighed. Then he turned round and climbed all the way down again. He worked his way through the grass and began to climb the willow herb. It was a very long way and he got quite out of breath.

Then, just as he was nearly there, Bumble Bee flew away again. Snail was so exasperated, that he forgot to hold on and fell... right into a big purple thistle flower.

"B-z-z-z! You're in my way. B-z-z-z-z-m!" And there was Bumble Bee.

"Have you seen Caterpillar's cabbage?" panted Snail, as quickly as he could.

"Um-m-m! It's by the truck with a lot of other cabbages," hummed Bumble Bee. "They are probably going to take it to market."

To market! So that was it.

Snail's heart sank. He knew that no-one who was taken to market ever came back home again.

"I must find her and warn her," he said. "I must hurry!"

"I'll show you where she is. Come along," buzzed Bumble Bee, and flew away.

"Oh dear," sighed Snail, as he eased himself down the prickly thistle. "She has forgotten that I don't fly."

But he found a trail of pollen on the ground. Bumble Bee had put it there to show him the way.

"Oh, I was wrong," said Snail. "She didn't forget."

Snail set off along the trail. Inch by inch he hurried on.
But it was a terrible trail.

It twisted, it turned, it zig-zagged, it went round and round in circles.

and once it went all the way up the stalk of a willow herb and down the other side. Snail was beginning to feel dizzy—and very cross with Bumble Bee. But he had to follow the trail if he wanted to find Caterpillar.

Suddenly it went zigging and zagging over some rocks.

"Hm, *mountains* now. Quite unnecessary, I'm sure," grumbled Snail. But he pulled himself up the steep slopes, and eased himself along the narrow ledges.

"I must hurry," he said to himself over and over again.

At last the trail twisted and turned down on to a wide sandy path.

"Hm! A *desert* now!" But Snail didn't say any more because the sun was blazing down on him, and there was no shade anywhere.

For several hours he limped along, but still the trail zig-zagged into the distance in front of him. He was hot and very dry, and the sand tickled his throat, making him cough.

"This is getting serious," he thought. "I'll dry out, and that'll be the end of me." Besides, Blackbird might see him out in the open.

"No, I really can't go any further," thought Snail. "I'll probably be too late anyway."

But, if Caterpillar was taken to market, she would never become a butterfly, and that would be a pity. Snail nibbled a weed that was growing between two pebbles.

"Perhaps I *can* go a little further," he thought.

Then suddenly, in the middle of nowhere, the trail stopped. Bumble Bee had run out of pollen. So that was that. There was nothing Snail could do now.

But, wait a minute! What was that smell blowing towards him? Snail set off again, very quickly.

It was the smell of cabbage!

Now the smell was easy to follow. It didn't zig-zag like Bumble Bee's trail. And in less than five minutes Snail had found the cabbages. They were packed in a crate, and there was an enormous truck waiting nearby.

"B-z-z-z-z-z-m! There you are at last, Snail." Bumble Bee zoomed up. "What *have* you been doing all this time? Do you never hurry?"

Never hurry! But Snail *had* hurried–every inch of the way. It had been a long and dangerous journey for a snail.

"Listen, Bumble Bee," he panted sternly. "If you had made a straight trail, I would have been here hours ago."

"B-z-z-z-z!" said Bumble Bee crossly and flew away. But a few moments later she was back again.

"I had to collect the pollen for the trail, didn't I? B-z-z-z-z-z! You old slow-coach!" and she flew away again.

Snail climbed up the crate calling, "Caterpillar! Caterpillar!"

There wasn't a sound from any of the cabbages. He began to wonder if Caterpillar had already gone, when, at last, he saw her peeping over a leaf. Her hair was standing on end, and she was shaking all over.

"Oh, Snail, I *am* glad to see you. I've been so frightened. That terrible wasp has been buzzing around for hours. She wouldn't go away! Thank goodness I had my cabbage to hide in. Wasps, you know, are my worst enemies."

"But that wasn't a wasp," explained Snail. "That was Bumble Bee. She wouldn't hurt you. She came to tell you that your house isn't safe any more."

"Of course it's safe. It's comfortable too–*and* nourishing."

As kindly as he could Snail began to tell Caterpillar the bad news.

"You mustn't be upset or frightened," he began. "But–"

Caterpillar wasn't listening.

"Why don't *you* live in a nice safe cabbage, Snail?" she chattered on. "Instead of wandering about like you do. One day Blackbird will catch you and bash..."

Suddenly Snail was very angry.

"*They are taking your cabbage to market!*" he shouted.

Caterpillar curled herself into a tight ball and dropped down beside him.

"Come along quickly!" she gasped and disappeared over the side of the crate. Snail turned round to follow her...but he was too late. Before he knew what was happening, the crate of cabbages was lifted on to the truck. There was a lot of banging and shaking, and then the truck began to move. He was being taken to market.

Poor Snail! He would never see the woods, the cabbage patch or any of his friends again. Miserably he sat and munched the crisp green leaves.

It was then that a dark shadow fell across Snail and the cabbages.

Blackbird! Snail shrunk into his shell just as Blackbird swooped, snatched him up in his beak and flew off towards his nest in the beech-tree.

This was worse than being taken to market! For the moment Snail was safe, curled up in his shell, but he knew that Blackbird was going to drop him, smash his shell, and eat him. This is, of course, what Blackbird meant to do, but things happened quite differently.

To get to his nest in the beech-tree he had to fly over the cabbage patch and past the cherry-tree. The cherry-tree was covered in ripe red cherries, and it was this that saved Snail.

Just for one moment Blackbird forgot all about him and stretched out to peck at one of the cherries. And, when he opened his beak, Snail toppled out and went hurtling down to the ground.

Down, down, down...

Spider had been spinning busily all day, and her web was finished. Now she only had to sit in her house and wait for a nice fat fly to get tangled up in the sticky threads. She kept her foot on a long silk line that was tied by the other end to the web. Suddenly the line shook.

"Aha!" she thought. "A fly!"

Then it shook again. She rubbed her feet together greedily.

"I must go and see what I have caught."

But when she saw that there wasn't a fly in her web–only Snail bouncing gently up and down–she went black with rage.

"I don't want that snail in my web," she squawked. She ran on to the web and cut a hole in it with her sharp claws. Snail slipped through the hole and landed gently on a leaf below.

He kept very still. He wasn't safe yet. He could hear Blackbird flying in and out of the cherry-tree.

Then at last he peeped cautiously out of his shell. Up above his head Spider sat mending her web. Everything was quiet and it was getting dark. Blackbird had flown home. He knew he couldn't find Snail once it was dark.

Snail was very, very tired now. All he wanted was to creep under some wet leaves, shut himself in his house and go to sleep. Slowly he crawled along the branch of the cherry-tree to the wall and up into a crack between the bricks.

The smell of wet leaves was blowing into the crack. "Not far now," he thought.

But just then he heard a little sob. He stopped and listened. There it was again. A little sob and then a shiver.

It was Caterpillar.

"Oh, oh, oh," she sobbed. "I have nowhere to live. I've been round and round the cabbage patch and there isn't a cabbage left. I've never been away from my cabbage before. Oh, what shall I do?"

Snail looked at Caterpillar. Dusty and bedraggled, she looked more like a curled-up leaf than a caterpillar.

"Come along,, he said. "I'll find you a home."

"But I just can't go another step," sobbed Caterpillar.

"Get on my back then," said Snail. "But keep in the middle and don't wriggle about, or I'll topple over."

So Caterpillar climbed on to Snail's shell and he set off towards the woods. He moved so smoothly that she soon fell fast asleep. And she didn't wake up until at last he stopped.

She opened her eyes, and there, beside the big beech-tree, and nearly hidden in the bracken, was a cabbage.

"It's old and ramshackle," said Snail. "But it *is* a cabbage, and it will be safe."

"It's beautiful," sighed Caterpillar. "It's even got flowers on it."

Caterpillar soon settled into her new home. When she put her head out to say "Goodnight" to Snail she was quite cheerful again.

"Oh, Snail," she called down. "I've been thinking. You haven't really got a home, have you? Why don't *you* live in a cabbage? They're safe and comfortable, and very nourishing..."

But Snail didn't listen. He *had* a home. It was on his back, and that was the very best place for a home. He crawled under some wet leaves. Then he crept into his shell and curled up comfortably.

Yes, he could wander all over the world, and when he needed it–wherever he was–his home was always there.